NOTHING BETWEEN FRIENDS

WRITTEN AND ILLUSTRATED BY
LEE TODD LACKS

Edited by Xtina Marie

A HellBound Books Publishing LLC Book
Houston TX

**A HellBound Books LLC
Publication**

Copyright © 2018 by HellBound Books Publishing LLC
All Rights Reserved

www.hellboundbookspublishing.com

Printed in the United States of America

ACKNOWLEDGMENTS

The illustration, "June Sans Culotte", was first published in *Vine Leaves Literary Journal,* Volume 17, November 2017

"Rue Sainte-Michelle" was first published in Vine *Leaves Literary Journal,* Volume 17, November 2017

"A Mother's Blessing" was first published in *Gold Dust Magazine,* Issue 30, February 2017

"Saint Michelle and the Offertory Font" was inspired by Natty's short story entitled "The Patron Saint of Spanking," which was an entry in the *2002 Soc.Sexuality.Spanking Summer Short Story Contest*

NOTHING BETWEEN FRIENDS

TABLE OF CONTENTS

RUE SAINTE-MICHELLE

Pleas of soundly
chastened brides
echo through the registers.

Ghosts of bygone
lingerie
lament in scented drawers.

Sisters blush at
either end
when blistered with the hairbrush.

Yardsticks sting the
upturned rumps
of shameless company girls.

A MOTHER'S BLESSING

Nancy had nine grown daughters,
as naughty as they were fair.
She knit them matching bloomers
with a plea upon each pair.

"If you should take this willful bride
to lay her bottom bare.
Please think it through before you do,
and paddle her with care.".

SAINT MICHELLE AND THE OFFERTORY FONT

Saint Michelle was born into a poor but loving family, who lived near the southern coast of France.

When she was nine years old, a clerk from the royal court came to her family's home collecting taxes for the king. Since taxes were unreasonably high at the time, Michelle's father did not have enough to pay. The clerk thus decreed that unless Michelle's father could pay by the end of the week, he would have him thrown into debtor's prison.

That night, the little girl prayed fervently, invoking the aid of the Blessed Virgin.

The next morning, as always, Michelle and her family went to Mass at Saint Genevieve's Church, which was just down the road from where they lived. Upon entering the church, Michele noticed a round receptacle fashioned from polished granite, about the size of a large wash basin, which served as an offertory font. Here, parishioners could give as much as they could spare to help those who were less fortunate. Michelle could see that it was veritably overflowing with all sorts of copper and silver coins.

For the remainder of the day, Michelle couldn't stop thinking about the pool of wealth in the offertory, and so, that night, after her mother and father lay fast asleep, the young girl crept out of the house, in nothing but her nightshift, and wandered down the road to Saint Genevieve's. Knowing that the church was never locked, Michelle quietly slipped through the front door to find no one else inside.

Upon approaching the offertory, Michelle's heart grew heavy as her eyes grew wide. "This money is meant for the poor," she thought. "Well, who could be poorer than we?"

With her guilt temporarily assuaged, she knelt down upon the hard tile floor and leaned over the broad beveled rim of the font. Reaching with both hands, she plunged into the coins, leaning further and further forward so that her arms were nearly submerged, and her bottom was fully upended. Having grabbed as many coins as she could possibly hold, Michelle attempted to withdraw from the font, when she suddenly realized that her hands were stuck fast. Panicking, she began to pull with all her might, but the harder she pulled, the more entrapped she became. Just then, a sudden gust of wind blew through the church, lifting Michelle's nightshift up over her bottom.

That same moment, she heard a soothing voice, "Oh, my naughty child - what am I going to do with you?" Michelle immediately recognized the voice as being that of the Blessed Mother, who was indeed standing behind her, bearing a birch rod.

"Holy Mary, please help me!" cried the frightened girl, bursting into tears.

"I shall," replied the Blessed Mother, but you know what needs to happen first?"

"Yes, Blessed Mother. I have sinned!" With that, Michelle's cries rang throughout the empty church as Mary put the rod to her bare bottom.

Overcome with sorrow, the little penitent began to fill the font with her tears. When the Blessed Mother had finally finished administering Michelle's punishment, she spoke to her tenderly. "My sweet Michelle, trust that your father will have what he needs."

"Thank you, Blessed Mother!" Michelle exclaimed as she wept for joy, "but, how will I get free?"

"Open your hands, my child." Mary replied.

Michelle did as she was told, letting go of the coins that

she had held so tightly, at which point, her arms were released from the font.

Having bid farewell to the Blessed Mother, she noticed that the birch rod now lay at her feet. Michelle picked it up reverently, and hurried home before her parents awoke, a sore but happy girl.

Later than morning, her father discovered a small bag of silver coins upon his workbench, which seemed to have miraculously appeared from out of nowhere.

In honor of the Blessed Mother's intervention, Michelle vowed to pay a perpetual penance.

Each and every night thereafter, she dutifully presented her parents with the birch rod, beseeching them to punish her for attempting to rob the church, and to this very day, whenever a storm looms off the coast, the fishwives warn that Saint Michelle is due for another whipping.

They say that lightning flashes each time the birch rod stings her bottom, thunder crashes in sympathy with the heaving of her sobs, and rain comes down in torrents from the falling of her tears.

STOCKING FEET

On Saturday, Trixie went to visit her dearest friend, June, who lived on the other side of Bangor. After chatting for the better part of an afternoon, the two ladies decided to look through some old photo albums. June invited her friend to follow her up the stairs 'til they came to a modestly appointed spare bedroom. Upon entering, Trixie immediately recognized the double bed from June's childhood home on Marsh Street. June's parents had given it to her when she and Roy first got married.

Having retrieved the albums, June carefully placed them near the foot of the bed. Then, they both proceeded to slip off their shoes and climb onto the mattress, laying side by side so that their stocking feet could rest upon the pillows. Once Trixie had assumed a comfortable position, she let her hands run along the chenille fabric of the bedspread, which she also recognized from the old house. Her mind began to wander as she plucked at the countless nibs on the spread.

"So, what is it that you're trying to get at, Trixie?" June inquired. The feel and scent of the heirloom quilt had taken her to a warm summer night some nine years prior, when she and June had found themselves in a very similar position, albeit under far less pleasant circumstances...

On the night in question, Trixie was staying over with June, as she often did when they were growing up. It so happened that they had both been invited to a party at Belinda Mae Thompson's house, and June's father had agreed to let them both go, provided that they returned by 11:00 PM. Suffice to say, the two friends had more than their fair share of fun that night, and by the time either of them bothered to check the clock in Belinda Mae's kitchen, it was nearly one o'clock in the morning. For as debaucherous as their evening had been, both young ladies knew to expect a firm reprimand when they got back to June's house. Sure enough, Mr. and Mrs. Jenkins were waiting in the living room, ready to confront them as soon as they walked through the door. Mr. Jenkins could hardly hold his temper as he asked his dallying daughter and her best friend whether or not they were alright.

When they each answered affirmatively, he told them to get upstairs. Trixie and June had both worn pink linen dresses that evening, with Mary Jane heels and sheer nylon stockings. Trixie recalled how she and June had stumbled tipsily up the stairs, stepping out of their heels the moment they set foot inside June's bedroom.

When Mr. Jenkins came up a few minutes later, he made a point of leaving the door wide open. "Why weren't you both home by eleven o'clock?" he questioned.

Try as they might to explain, neither June nor Trixie could offer a reasonable testimony. "We're sorry, Papa." June apologized repeatedly. "We were having so much fun at Belinda Mae's party that we lost all track of time!"

"Have you two been drinkin'?" Mr. Jenkins asked, his tone becoming alarmingly familiar.

"Um..um..maybe just a little." Trixie blurted out, regretting the words even as she uttered them.

"Well, that settles it. I've heard enough! June, if you thought you were too old for the strap, think again, because you're gonna get it!

"No, Papa! Please! Not that!" June wailed. "I haven't gotten the strap in over a year!"

"That's right, young lady, but until I can trust you to do what I say, you're gonna get it every week!

"Papa!!"

"M..Mr. Jenkins," Trixie interjected. "It's not June's fault. I'm the one who made us late! June kept tellin' me it was time to go home, but I kept draggin' my feet."

"Is that so, Trixie Ann? Well, I admire your honesty, and since you've been such a good friend to June, I'm gonna strap you right alongside her."

"B..but, Mr. Jenkins!"

"Trixie," June's father continued, "From the time you and June were knee-high to a grasshopper, your father and I agreed that if either of you misbehaved while you were under our care, we would punish you like we punish our own."

"B..but, Mr. Jenkins. That was a long time ago." Trixie protested, unable to think of a more adequate defense.

"Would you prefer that I call him, Trixie?"

"No, sir, please..don't!" the fretful girl beseeched, knowing full well that if her father ever found out that she had kept Mr. and Mrs. Jenkins up past midnight waiting for her to return from a party, he would march over and spank her himself!

"Please don't punish us, Papa!" June pleaded, hoping against hope that her father might reconsider his decision. June had just turned 19 that summer, and the thought of being strapped alongside her best friend seemed utterly mortifying.

"Not another word!" Mr. Jenkins admonished his grown daughter. "Now then, ladies, you both know the drill. Get your skirts up, and your drawers down! I don't want to see anything between you and this belt."

Trixie could see June's mother standing in the doorway, alternately cringing and nodding in approval; the fact that

Mrs. Jenkins was still subject to the strap remained one of the worst kept secrets in Bangor.

Despite their abject protests, June and Trixie did as they were told, tearfully baring their bottoms before laying face down upon the bed.

Trixie shuddered to recall the awful *thwack* of the belt, as it stung each of their rear ends in turn. The steady cadence of the strap was soon accompanied by the anguished percussion of stocking feet, drumming the bed in despair.

"Trixie? Trixie! Anybody home?!" June's insistent voice slung her friend back to reality.

"Oh...umm...I'm sorry...which photo were we looking at?" she faltered, vainly attempting to conceal her chagrin.

"What's gotten in to you, girl?" June asked perplexedly. Just then, Trixie noticed her legs thrashing against the mattress. "From the way you're carryin' on, I'd swear you were bein' spanked!" As Trixie struggled to regain her composure, June gave her a good-natured swat on the behind.

"Owww!! Damn it, June! That hurts!" cried her friend, grinning conspiratorially until they both laughed out loud...

NOTHING BETWEEN FRIENDS
(A Play in Three Acts)

Characters

Trixie LaFleur: A woman in her late twenties

June Jenkins: Trixie's best friend; also in her late twenties

Father Allen: A Roman Catholic priest in his late sixties

Eileen Lenehan: A woman in her mid sixties who leads the Sacred Sisterhood of Flidais

The Sisterhood: A secret society of pagan women from all walks of life who have devoted themselves to Flidais, the Celtic goddess of animals, woodlands, and fertility.

ACT ONE

TIME: An afternoon in April 1963

SETTING: The guest bedroom in a saltbox cottage belonging to JUNE and her husband, located on the East Side of Bangor, Maine

The play opens with TRIXIE, and her best friend, JUNE, lying prone upon a double bed looking through some old photo albums.

TRIXIE
Oh, June. These pictures are priceless!

JUNE
I thought you'd appreciate them!
(turning the page of the album, and suddenly pointing to a black-and-white photo of TRIXIE in what appears to be a floor-length gown)
Oh, look at this one, Trixie!

TRIXIE
(mildly embarrassed)
Oh, my!

                    JUNE
     That was the night of your senior prom!

                   TRIXIE
              (a bit sheepish)
                    Ayuh.

                    JUNE
      Oh, my God. Look at that dress!
                 (tenderly)
            You looked beautiful.

                   TRIXIE
             Aw..Thanks, hon.

                    JUNE
                 Why, sure!

                   TRIXIE
     I still remember riding home with Timmy
             Flanagan that night.

                    JUNE
                (giggling)
     Well, as I recall, you two didn't exactly
             head straight home.

                   TRIXIE
                (blushing)
               No, we didn't.

                    JUNE
     I still can't believe you drove out to the
                   slip!

                    TRIXIE
          Ayuh, to..um..admire the view.

                     JUNE
                   (laughing)
         Yeah, right! How was the view from the
              backseat of Timmy's car?

                    TRIXIE
                  (blushing)
      Oh, my God, June. Thank you for reminding
      me. I always wondered why they called that
                 place the slip.

                     JUNE
            (grinning mischievously)
         Well, things certainly had a way of
                slippin' off there.

                    TRIXIE
              ..and slippin' *in*.

                     JUNE
         (covers her mouth with her hands)
                 Trixie Ann!!

                    TRIXIE
                  (giggling)
       Timmy and I were barely dressed when
            Officer Quinn caught us.

                     JUNE
                So, I've heard!

                    TRIXIE
        I *begged* him not to call my parents.

                    JUNE
                  (teasing)
              But, he *did!*

                    TRIXIE
              (sighing ruefully)
        Ayuh, and by the time they were
     through with me, my rear end was redder
               than my lipstick!

Both ladies burst out laughing.

                    JUNE
     Ayuh, you sure had a knack for gettin' in
                  trouble, Trix!

                    TRIXIE
                  (sheepish)
                 I sure did.

                    JUNE
       I still remember your little sister,
     Kerry, asking you why you couldn't sit the
                  next morning!

Both resume laughing.

                    TRIXIE
     Well, gettin' in trouble isn't *all* bad.

                    JUNE
                  (giggling)
     Yeah, as long as you don't get caught!

                   TRIXIE
                  (impish)
     Oh, I don't know. Sometimes, gettin'
            caught is half the fun.

                    JUNE
      Sure, if your idea of havin' fun is a
             well-seared rear end!

                   TRIXIE
         (grinning mischievously)
           So...what if it is?

                    JUNE
                (taken aback)
                  Trixie!

                   TRIXIE
     June, can I share a secret with you?

                    JUNE
                   Sure.

                   TRIXIE
     Promise me you won't tell *anyone*.

                    JUNE
          (crossing her fingers)
                I promise.

TRIXIE
Well, you remember how our parents used to
spank us all the time when were growing
up?

JUNE
(a bit apprehensive)
Um..yeah. How could I forget?

TRIXIE
I know this is gonna sound crazy, but
there were times when I almost... enjoyed
it.

JUNE
Are you kiddin' me?!

TRIXIE
No, I'm not. I've never understood why,
but sometimes, when I was feeling *really*
naughty, the idea of being spanked seemed
kind of comforting. Did it ever seem that
way to you?

JUNE
What?! Oh, God, no! I hated it! That's why
I tried to so hard to be good all the
time. How could you have enjoyed bein'
spanked?!

TRIXIE
Well, I think a lot of it had to do with
letting go of the guilt.

                         JUNE
          I don't understand. What do you mean?

                        TRIXIE
         You know, like, when you're sick, and you
          need to get something out of your system?

                         JUNE
           Kind of like that time we all got food
             poisonin' from Nana Nancy's quahog
                        chowdah?

                        TRIXIE
                     (acquiescent)
                     Um..kind of.

                         JUNE
      Oh, my God, I've nevah had such awful stomach cramps!

                        TRIXIE
        (resigned to her friend's indelicate analogy)
         You and me both. We were on the toilet all night.

                         JUNE
                       (sighing)
         Ayuh... takin' turns and prayin' for relief.

TRIXIE
(wryly)
Lead us not into the bathroom, but deliver us from Pepto Bismol.

JUNE
(in unison with TRIXIE)
Amen.

JUNE
You know, that may be the only time in my life I've ever prayed on the toilet.

TRIXIE
(still laughing)
Desperate times call for desperate measures, Junie. Seriously though, do you remember when your cramps were about to..run their course?

JUNE
(blushing profusely)
Trixie Ann! What kind of a question is that?!

TRIXIE
(sheepish)
Well?

JUNE
(exasperated)
Why yes, Trixie. I felt like my insides were comin' loose! Couldn't you hear me cheerin' from the bathroom?!

TRIXIE
(*giggling*)
Oh, I heard you.

JUNE
(*suddenly embarrassed*)
You *didn't*.

TRIXIE
Ayuh..right before you turned into an
upside-down volcano.

Uproarious laughter ensues.

JUNE
(*chagrined*)
Oh, my God, Trixie!! That's disgusting!!

TRIXIE
(*still laughing*)
I'm sorry, hon, but didn't you feel so
much better, afterwards?

JUNE
Eeewww! I can't believe we're talkin'
about this!!

TRIXIE
Come on, now. Didn't you?

JUNE
Well, of course I did! I don't know when
I've ever felt so relieved!

                    TRIXIE
       Me neither, but that's exactly how I felt
        whenever our parents spanked us. For as
         heavy as the punishments might have
        seemed, they made my spirit feel that much
                     lighter.

                     JUNE
    Oh, yeah? Well, they made my backside feel
                 that much sorer!

Both resume laughing.

                     JUNE
              (suddenly earnest)
        Trixie, why did you feel guilty all the
                      time?

                    TRIXIE
               (hesitantly)
          Do you *really* want to know?

                     JUNE
            Yes. Please tell me.

                    TRIXIE
     (after a long pause, in a hushed voice)
          Because, I believe in spirits.

                     JUNE
        You mean, like, the Holy Spirit?

                    TRIXIE
               No, not exactly.

                    JUNE
         You mean like, Mémé Genevieve?

                   TRIXIE
      Oh, I believe in her, alright - but that's
      not what I mean. I mean, like, the moon
             and the sun and the stars.

                    JUNE
        Well, I don't see anything wrong with
           admirin' the wonders of Nature.

                   TRIXIE
      Yeah, I know, June, but I..worship them.

                    JUNE
        What do you mean, you *worship* them?

                   TRIXIE
      I worship the nature spirits. The sun, the
      moon, the forest, the ocean, all living
           things. You see... I'm a pagan.

                    JUNE
                  A what?!?!

                   TRIXIE
      I'm a *pagan*. I serve the dominion of
                   Flidais.

                    JUNE
        What in the world is Flidais?!

TRIXIE
(with reverence)
She's the Celtic goddess of
animals, woodlands, and fertility.

JUNE
(half-joking)
The goddess?! Trixie Ann La Fleur, I
oughta put you over my knee for utterin'
such heresy.

TRIXIE
I knew I shouldn't have told you! You're
still turnin' on me, just like you did
when we were growin' up!

JUNE
Well, it seems you still have a lot of
growin' up to do!

TRIXIE
(offended)
How can you say that?!

JUNE
(derisively)
Come on, Trixie. Admit it. You're still
runnin' around the backyahd in your fairy
costume, pretendin' you can talk to the
animals.

TRIXIE
No, you're wrong! There's so much more to it
than that! Serving the Lady of the Forest is
my sacred calling.

JUNE
*(recognizing the gravity of TRIXIE'S
admission)*
Holy Mother of God, Trixie...You're not
kiddin', are you?

TRIXIE
(fraught with emotion)
No, I'm not. Pagan is what I am.

JUNE
(becoming angry)
Do you mean to tell me that my best friend,
who was raised to believe in The Ten
Commandments, spends her free time traipsin'
through the forest, prayin' to false gods?!

TRIXIE
(in tears)
June, you don't understand! I tried to
resist! For years, I tried! I always thought
that if I got punished enough, someday, I'd
eventually stop believing in them, but I
just couldn't pretend to be a Christian
anymore! It seems so natural! If people say
that God created the Earth, and everything
within it, then why is it such a sin for
someone to worship those things?!

JUNE watches TRIXIE sob for nearly a minute.

                    JUNE
          (with measured compassion)
     Trixie, I may not understand it, and I
     certainly don't condone it, but you're my
       best friend, and that's never gonna
                   change.

TRIXIE embraces JUNE and resumes sobbing.

                   TRIXIE
                (whimpering)
             I love you, June.

                    JUNE
          I love you, too, Trixie.
               (her eyes darken)
     So..being spanked helped to ease your
                conscience, huh?

                   TRIXIE
                (vulnerably)
             Well... yeah.

                    JUNE
     Do you remember my Mom's hairbrush?

                   TRIXIE
                (blushing)
               I sure do.

                    JUNE
Well, I went to the estate sale for Maggie
   Lenehan on Saturday, and I found this
  lovely antique hairbrush. It reminded me
   so much of Mom's. Maggie raised seven
 girls on her own, so you know the back of
    that brush has seen a lot of sorry
                 backsides.

                   TRIXIE
            (giggling nervously)
              I can only imagine.

                    JUNE
       Yes, I'm excited to try it out.

                   TRIXIE
            Um..what do you mean?

                    JUNE
  Well, if I'm gonna be a mama someday, I
  need to try my hand at spankin' naughty
                  girls.

                   TRIXIE
              Wait..um..what?

                    JUNE
  You said that being spanked helped to
       lighten your spirit, right?

                   TRIXIE
            Well, yeah... but...

JUNE
(smiling)
Well, by the time I'm through with you,
your spirit's gonna be floatin' off the
ground.

TRIXIE
(alarmed)
June, you can't be serious.

JUNE
Oh, I'm quite serious, Trixie. I'm gonna
spank you, and you're gonna let me, that
is unless you want all of Bangor to know
about your *calling.*

TRIXIE
No, June! Please don't!

JUNE
Alright, then I expect your full
cooperation.

TRIXIE
June, please!

JUNE
Would you prefer that I call your parents?

TRIXIE
(despairs in recognition of the catch-22)
Nooooo!!

(CONT'D)

                    JUNE
You should be grateful that I'm the only
one who knows, Trixie. Can you imagine
what your Mom and Dad would do if they
            ever found out?

                   TRIXIE
          (dreading the thought)
                  N..no.

                    JUNE
Why, I bet your Dad would put you back
over the front fence, with your rear end
        facing the street this time.

                   TRIXIE
               (shudders)

                    JUNE
Ayuh, I bet that's just what he'd do.
Then, he'd have a cookout on the front
lawn, and invite all the neighbors, and
when they asked, "Why is Trixie Ann draped
over the fence with her skirts up in the
air?" he'd tell them about your heathen
practice, and ask them to pray for you
while he strapped your bare behind.
           (suddenly cheerful)
Now, if you'll excuse me, I'm going to get
              my hairbrush.

JUNE *exits* *the* *room,* *leaving* *TRIXIE* *to* *fret* *over* *the* *most* *humiliating* *punishment* *either* *of* *them* *had* *ever* *endured.* *She* *returns* *a* *few* *moments* *later,* *toting* *a* *hefty wooden paddle brush.*

                    JUNE
    (gently tapping the brush against her left
                    palm)
Now then, young lady. Go ahead and hike up
                that dress.

                   TRIXIE
                (mortified)
            June, no!!

                    JUNE
            You heard me!

Despairingly, *TRIXIE* *reaches* *down* *to* *grab* *the* *hem* *of* *her* *swing* *dress,* *lifting* *it* *to* *reveal* *the* *seafoam* *green* *panties* *that* *she* *wore* *beneath* *her* *sheer* *to* *waist* *nylons.* *JUNE* *climbs* *up* *onto* *the* *bed* *and* *extends* *her* *right* *leg* *so* *that* *her* *foot* *nearly* *touches* *the* *footboard.* *She* *then* *tucks* *her* *left leg off to the side.*

                    JUNE
            (patting the mattress)
        Get over here, Trixie.

TRIXIE
June, please! There has to be a better
way!

JUNE
Trixie, I'm sorry. You're absolutely
right. How can I paddle your rear end
properly if I don't let you bare it? Take
down your underwear, please.

TRIXIE
Oh, my God, June! No! That's not what I
mean!

JUNE
Do it, now!

*Slipping her fingers inside the waistbands
of her pantyhose and panties, TRIXIE tugs
them down below her knees. She then
hobbles over to the bed, and lays prone
across the mattress, so that her thighs
rest upon JUNE'S upper right leg. JUNE
then proceeds to thread her left leg
between TRIXIE'S knees, just above the
tangle of her underwear, effectively
pinning her friend's right leg. As JUNE
shifts to gain greater leverage, her skirt
rides up past the point of discretion.*

JUNE
(teasing *TRIXIE'S backside with the
hairbrush*)
There you go... So, tell me, naughty girl.
How do you honor these false gods of
yours?

**Aroused by shame, and shamed by arousal,
TRIXIE resigns herself to her friend's
twisted judgment.**

TRIXIE
They're not false, June!

**JUNE gives TRIXIE four sharp swats on the
rear end.**

JUNE
If they aren't the Father, the Son, and
the Holy Spirit, then they're *false*,
Trixie!

TRIXIE
(*crying out*)
Owwwww!! Noooo! Flidais is wonderful! She
looks after the animals, she makes the
trees grow, she brings new life in the
Spring...

JUNE
(*gives TRIXIE four more swats*)
No, Trixie! God does all that!

                         TRIXIE
                  (crying out louder)
         Ooowwwww!! But, what if Flidais and God
                    work together?

                          JUNE
         God's not a holdin' company, Trixie! He
                doesn't need extra help!

                         TRIXIE
                  But what if, June?!

                          JUNE
                 (continues spanking)
         Yes, what if, Trixie! What if God were to
         strike you down, right here and now, for
                denyin' His mighty works?!

                         TRIXIE
                   (in acute distress)
                 Junie, don't say that!!

**JUNE proceeds to apply firm, deliberate
strokes with the hairbrush.**

                          JUNE
         So, how do you honor this Flidais?

                         TRIXIE
                  (gasping out the words)
         She..requires me..to..share my..intimacy!

JUNE
*(relenting just long enough for TRIXIE to
explain herself)*
Your intimacy?

TRIXIE
Yes.

JUNE
How do you share your intimacy?

TRIXIE
I..I can't tell you. It's
a..secret..ritual.

JUNE
(becoming angry again)
You either tell me, or you tell your Mom
and Dad!

TRIXIE
No, no! Please! I'll tell you!

JUNE
Go on.

TRIXIE
(hesitating)
Well..

JUNE
*(bringing the brush down with renewed
fervor)*
Out with it!

                    TRIXIE
          (flailing her legs in pain)
    Alright! Alright! Each month, between
    March and November, I have to go out into
    the woods and find a mayapple. Once I find
    it, I cut the root from the stalk, wash it
    off in the pond, and take it to a sacred
    place, where no one can see me. Then...

                    JUNE
    *(gives her TRIXIE several more resounding
                    smacks)*
              Then, what?

                    TRIXIE
    *(absurdly fast, so as to render her speech
            nearly incomprehensible)*
    I reach up my skirt, take down my panties,
    and slide the root between my legs until
              it makes me tingle.
                 (flinches)

                    JUNE
            (terrifyingly calm)
              Oh, is that all?

                    TRIXIE
    (taken aback by JUNE'S nonchalance)
    Well, um..then, I take it out, bury it in
    the ground, and say some prayers.

JUNE
*(emphasizing the boldfaced words with
strokes of the hairbrush)*
I see. So, let me get this straight. You
go **out into** the **woods, drop** your **drawers**
in **broad daylight,** pleasure yourself with
a **poisonous plant,** and **offer** it to some
pagan effigy?!

↑
Simultaneously
↓

TRIXIE
(in dire distress)
Oooowww! Ooowwww! Ooowwwww! Pleeeease,
Juuuunie!! No more!! Ooooooohhh, that
hurts! Ooowwww!! No more, Juuunie!
Pleeeease!! Ooooowwwww!! I won't do it
again! I promise! Ooooowwwww!! I promise!!

JUNE
(outraged)
You have sinned against the Lord, Trixie Ann!!

TRIXIE
(tearfully regressing)
I know, Juuunie!! I..b..been naughty!! S..so naughty!!

JUNE
(spanking in time with the first three words)
Yes, you have, and what do naughty girls need?!

                              TRIXIE
              Oooooowwwww! Naughty girls need mo' spankin'!

                               JUNE
                            (solemnly)
            That's right, Trixie Ann, so what do you need?!

                              TRIXIE
                    (anguished yet aroused)
                      I need mo' spankin'!

                               JUNE
                          Say it again.

                              TRIXIE
                   (regressing even further)
        ..I need m..mo' spankin'! Pleeeease! I've..b..been a naughty
        girl!! S..such a..n..naughty girl!! P..p..pleeease, give me
                mo' spankin', Juuunie!! Pleeeeasse!!

**JUNE pauses to examine TRIXIE'S bottom, cringing at the myriad
of welts that distress its broad expanse.**

                               JUNE
               (calmly but firmly after a long pause)
        Be careful what you ask for, Trixie, because I'm about to give
                 you another twenty with the brush.

                              TRIXIE
                    (having second thoughts)
                      Oh, my God! *Twenty?!*

                              JUNE
                        You asked for it.

As *JUNE* administers the remainder of *TRIXIE'S* punishment, *TRIXIE'S* cries of anguish morph into lascivious moans.

                              JUNE
                    (with mock indignation)
                    Trixie Ann! Shame on you!

                             TRIXIE
                          (mortified)
                  Uuunnnooo!! No! Junie, please!

                              JUNE
                       (in a firmer tone)
                    Are you *enjoying* this?!

                             TRIXIE
                    (woefully unconvincing)
                            Noooo!

                              JUNE
              Oh, my God..you are! You sinful, sinful girl!

                             TRIXIE
                  Nooooo, Juuunie! Pleeeease!!

                              JUNE
        Please, what?! Please paddle your rear end...............until
                    you beg for forgiveness?!

                    TRIXIE
        (rushing past the point of no return)
                 Juuuuunieee!!

                     JUNE
                  (strident)
          That's what you want, isn't it?!

                    TRIXIE
                  Noooooo!

                     JUNE
           (spanking with fanatic zeal)
                  ISN'T IT?!

                    TRIXIE
           (climaxing involuntarily)
    OH, GOD!! YESSSSS!! YEESSSSSS!! YEEESSSSSSSS!!!

TRIXIE is reduced to a half-naked heap of spasms and sobs, soaking JUNE's lap with the release of her intimacy. JUNE bears silent witness for well over two minutes.

                     JUNE
               (at a loss for words)
             Jesus Christ, Trixie.

Inexplicably moved by TRIXIE'S undoing, JUNE caresses her friend's distended bottom as she cries herself out. Several more minutes pass before TRIXIE begins to regain her adulthood.

                    TRIXIE
                 (whimpering)
            I'm s..sorry, Junie.

                    JUNE
                (rhetorically)
I know you are, Trixie Ann, but are you sorry enough to have
          no other gods before the Lord?

                    TRIXIE
        (after an unbearably long pause)
            N..no, June. I..I'm not.
   (flinches in anticipation of further punishment)

                    JUNE
            (with mock resignation)
Very well, my friend, then you Had better plan on spendin'
         many more long afternoons over my lap.

                    TRIXIE
              (feigning distress)
                 W..what?!

                    JUNE
You heard me. Since you refuse to renounce this *goddess* of
yours, I will expect you to come here straight from work, each
and every Saturday, so that I can give you another spankin'.
                Is that clear?

                    TRIXIE
        (trying not to seem too pleased)
               Y..yes, Junie!

                         JUNE
      Alright, then... Straighten up your delicates, and get ready
                         for church.

                         TRIXIE
                         Okay.

*JUNE releases her hold upon TRIXIE'S right leg, thus enabling
her to get down from the bed. With her panties and pantyhose
still in a bunch, TRIXIE makes her way towards the upstairs
bathroom. JUNE stifles a laugh as she watches TRIXIE waddling
across the floor in her "stylish yet liberating" underwear.*

                         TRIXIE
           (moments later, from behind the bathroom door)
                       Hey, Junie!

                         JUNE
                         Yeah?

                         TRIXIE
                       (in earnest!)
      Can I go without underwear, just for tonight? My rear end's
                         killin' me.

                         JUNE
                      (admonishing)
                       Trixie Ann!

                         TRIXIE
                       (retracting)
                    Alright! Alright!

TRIXIE emerges a few minutes later with her dress and her delicates primly in place.

                              JUNE
                  (giving TRIXIE the once over)
That's better... Now, let's go. If we don't get to church by
            3:45, we won't be able to get a seat.

                             TRIXIE
                      (sighs ruefully)
     That's fine with me. I won't be sittin' anytime soon.

JUNE gives TRIXIE a gentle kiss on the forehead, and follows her out of the room.

ACT TWO

TIME: Approximately 3:00 PM on a Saturday, six months
                     later

SETTING: Inside Saint Michelle's Roman Catholic Church

Having spent yet another afternoon paddling TRIXIE'S behind, JUNE informs her friend that she plans to go to confession later that afternoon. TRIXIE offers to meet JUNE at the church so that they can attend Saturday evening Mass together. Upon arriving at St. Michelle's, JUNE enters the first open confessional, and draws the curtain behind her.

                          JUNE
             Bless me Father, for I have sinned

                       FATHER ALLEN
        How long has it been since your last confession?

                          JUNE
                       One week.

                       FATHER ALLEN
             How have you sinned, my child?

                          JUNE
I took the Lord's name in vain three times, I said a curse
word when I burned my hand on the teakettle last Tuesday, and
I lied to the salesgirl at Woolworth's when she asked if I had
                 worn the slip I was returning.

                      FATHER ALLEN
    I see. Is there anything more you'd like to tell me?

                          JUNE
            (after an uncomfortably long pause)
Yes, Father. I have been spanking my best friend every week,
                 for the past six months.

                      FATHER ALLEN
              I'm sorry. What did you say?

                          JUNE
I have been spanking my best friend every week, for the past
                     six months.

                      FATHER ALLEN
               How old is your friend?

                          JUNE
                   Twenty-eight.

                      FATHER ALLEN
Why, she's a grown woman. What could she possibly have done to
               provoke such treatment?

                          JUNE
She has broken one of the Commandments, and I fear for her
                        soul.

                    FATHER ALLEN
                Are you her guardian?

                        JUNE
                    No, Father.

                    FATHER ALLEN
    Then, you have no authority to discipline her. If your friend
        has sinned, then she must answer to God.

                        JUNE
                    Yes, Father.

                    FATHER ALLEN
                Is there anything more?

                        JUNE
                (choking back tears)
    Yes, Father..Soon after I started spanking this friend of
    mine, I noticed myself becoming.. physically aroused.

                    FATHER ALLEN
            (barely containing his outrage)
    So, you have been indulging in your friend's mortification for
                nearly six months?!

                        JUNE
                (weeping openly)
            Y..yes, Father! I have s..sinned!

                    FATHER ALLEN
    Indeed you have, young lady, and I'm afraid that saying a
        couple of Rosaries won't be enough to absolve you.

                              JUNE
                  (recognizing the insinuation)
                      I understand, Father.

                          FATHER ALLEN
        Very well, then. Please step out into the nave, and reflect
        upon the image of our church's patron saint. I'll be with you
                             shortly.

JUNE exits the confessional, breathing a sigh of relief when she discovers that TRIXIE has yet to arrive. Per FATHER ALLEN'S instructions, she follows the wall that runs along the epistle side of the church, until she comes to a niche, which houses a life-size marble statue of Saint Michelle bearing the proverbial rod of correction. As she contemplates the zeal with which Michelle embraced her penance, JUNE begins to notice herself trembling in the aisle. Unbeknownst to her, several ladies from the city clerk's office happen to be sitting in the pew immediately to her left. Upon observing their co-worker's visible distress, the ladies exchange empathetic glances and nods of tacit approval. Within a few minutes, FATHER ALLEN emerges from the confessional, dressed in the purple vestments customarily worn by priests during Lent. He proceeds to approach his anxious penitent.

                          FATHER ALLEN
                      (standing beside her)
                    Come with me, please.

                              JUNE
                        Yes, Father.

JUNE follows FATHER ALLEN towards the front of the church, stopping when they reach the altar rails. With a nod, the senior priest lets JUNE know that she may pass, at which point, she ascends the three stairs that lead to the sanctuary. Turning to her right, she continues to follow FATHER ALLEN through a door that opens into a large, well-appointed sacristy containing chalices, clerical vestments, and various other consecrated items. The two of them walk in silence towards the back of the room, towards a long and narrow staircase that leads to the undercroft of the church.

As JUNE and FATHER ALLEN descend these stairs, a strange and musty smell triggers some of her most painful childhood memories. The undercroft is essentially an expansive basement, with brick-lined walls and vaulted ceilings. The area is lit by dozens of intermittently spaced gas lamps. Upon reaching the bottom of the stairs, JUNE notices random articles of furniture that seem to have no particular purpose, all except for a solitary oaken kneeler that looms rather conspicuously some fifty yards in the distance. In addition to being unusually tall, the top shelf of this kneeler appears to be fully padded. Along a nearby wall, approximately fifteen feet beyond the kneeler, lies a small niche bearing an assortment of paddles and canes. Affixed to the wall just beneath this niche is a brass plate with a quote from Proverbs 13:24: "Whoever spares the rod hates their children, but the one who loves their children is careful to discipline them."

FATHER ALLEN
Tell me, June Marie Jenkins, how long has it been since you and I last met here?

JUNE
(quavering as she follows FATHER ALLEN towards the kneeler)
Oh, I can't recall, Father Allen. Fifteen years, at least.

FATHER ALLEN
Sounds about right. Well, some of God's children never seem to outgrow their need for the rod, now, do they?

JUNE
(dejectedly)
No, Father.

FATHER ALLEN
(sighing)
Mass begins in half an hour, so let's get this over with. Please prepare yourself.

JUNE wipes away a tear as she approaches the kneeler. While bending at the waist, she raises her skirt and slip to reveal the voluminous panty girdle that holds her nylon stockings in place. Having detached the garters of the girdle from her nylons, JUNE shimmies her way out of the constrictive undergarment, much to the vexation of FATHER ALLEN.

FATHER ALLEN
Up and over, please.

JUNE straddles the knee rest while pushing her hips against the padded shelf, purposefully presenting her bottom for correction. Moments later, FATHER ALLEN turns to the left wall and removes one of the heavier canes. He takes a few precursory swings before proceeding with JUNE'S penance.

FATHER ALLEN
Given the grievous nature of your sin, I'm going to give you fifteen with the cane, June.

                    JUNE
                  (gasping)
              Fifteen, Father?!

                 FATHER ALLEN
Yes, in order to keep you from taking carnal pleasure in your
friend's suffering, I must remind you what it's like to be on
                 the receiving end.

                    JUNE
                (whimpering)
          I... I understand, Father.

**FATHER ALLEN proceeds to walk behind JUNE. Moments later, JUNE
hears a dreadful thwack, as the cane sears her backside like a
white hot tongue of flame. Out in the nave, TRIXIE has just
arrived to find that the church is nearly full. She takes her
seat in a short pew towards the very back of the cavernous
church, when suddenly, she hears a very faint cry of anguish
emanating from a heating register in the floor beneath her
feet. As she listens to each and every subsequent cry, JUNE'S
bosom friend notices herself becoming inexplicably aroused.**

                 FATHER ALLEN
*(in a stern voice, just prior to delivering the fifteenth
                     stroke)*
  ..Do you repent for having subjected your dear friend to
             corporal punishment?

**Still doubled over the kneeler, JUNE whimpers incoherently,
having long since lost all capacity for response. FATHER ALLEN
pauses to examine the lattice of crimson welts that distend
her backside.**

                              JUNE
                          (anguished)
                        I..I do, Father!

                          FATHER ALLEN
And do you repent for having taken pleasure in her suffering?

                              JUNE
                           (wailing)
                             I do!

                          FATHER ALLEN
Then, I absolve you from your sins, in the name of the Father,
          the Son, and the Holy Ghost. Amen.

                              JUNE
                             Amen!

PAENITENTIAM

(CONT'D)

TRIXIE startles as JUNE lets go one last heartrending cry. FATHER ALLEN gives JUNE a few minutes to regain her composure and collect her underwear before proceeding to celebrate the Mass. In order to save her from any undue embarrassment, FATHER ALLEN lets JUNE leave through the sacristy so that she can go around the back of the church and re-enter through the vestibule. Less than ten minutes later, JUNE emerges from the vestibule to find TRIXIE waiting for her just inside the entrance. Relieved to see her friend, TRIXIE moves a few feet further into her pew so that JUNE can stand beside her.

TRIXIE
(whispering loudly)
Where have you been?!

JUNE
(dismissively)
I had to use the bathroom. My stomach's botherin' me.

TRIXIE
(genuinely concerned)
Are you okay?

JUNE
Yeah, I'll be fine.

As the opening hymn concludes, FATHER ALLEN enters the sanctuary with several other priests and deacons. He takes his place behind the altar, and commences with the Mass.

FATHER ALLEN
Please be seated.

JUNE shudders at the prospect of having to set her very sore backside upon the wooden bench of the pew.

JUNE
(moaning softly)
Oh, God.

TRIXIE
June, what's wrong? Is it your stomach?

JUNE
(in an exasperated whisper)
Shush, Trixie. I'll talk to you when we get outside.

Despite having to stand up and sit back down seven more times, JUNE manages to suffer through the Mass. As the congregation sings the final strains of the closing hymn, JUNE steps out into the aisle to let TRIXIE know that she is all too eager to leave.

JUNE
(hastily genuflecting)
Let's go.

TRIXIE
(knowing enough not to inquire)
Okay.

Having stepped outside, TRIXIE follows JUNE back to her house, which is located just a few blocks down from the church. They talk all along the way.

TRIXIE
How's your stomach?

JUNE
It'll be alright.

TRIXIE
You should be glad you were in the bathroom before Mass. Some poor girl was doin' her penance in the undercroft.

JUNE
(feigning surprise)
No! Really?!

TRIXIE
Ayuh. I heard her through a grate in the floor beneath my feet. The sound was very faint, but I could tell she was screamin' like a banshee!

JUNE
How many do you think she got?

TRIXIE
I counted fifteen.

JUNE
Fifteen! Holy Mother of God! She's not gonna be sittin' anytime soon, I can tell you that!

TRIXIE
Amen! Do you remember our mothers bringin' us to confession when we were little? I was always so scared whenever one of them had to go over the kneeler.

                          JUNE
        Oh, I remember. Your Mom used to say that Father Allen was
                      deliverin' her from evil.

                         TRIXIE
        Yeah. It took all I had not to go down there and save her.

                          JUNE
                  (dubious of TRIXIE'S motives)
                    You mean *pay her penance*?!

                         TRIXIE
                  (embarrassed by her transparency)
                        Well...yeah.

                          JUNE
        Yeah, well you know what would've happened then, don't you?

                         TRIXIE
                        (eagerly)
                        No, what?

                          JUNE
        Father Allen would've made you watch while he finished with
        her, and then, he would've hauled your naked rear end over
        that kneeler, and paddled you within an inch of your life.

                         TRIXIE
                        (wistfully)
                        Really?!

JUNE
And then, your mother would've dragged you out of there,
kickin' and screamin', and paddled you twice as hard as soon
as she got you home!

TRIXIE
(swooning)
Oooohh.

JUNE
(shaking her head)
Honest to God, Trixie.

As TRIXIE and JUNE turn onto Baylor Street, they can see JUNE'S house at the end of the block.

TRIXIE
Do you remember the last time you did your penance in the
undercroft, Junie?

JUNE
(with no affect)
Oh, it's been at least an hour.

TRIXIE
(stunned)
W...What?!?! Oh, my God!! That was you screamin' down
there?!?!

JUNE
Ayuh. I told Father Allen that I have been spankin' you every
week for the past six months, and he gave me a penance to
match.

TRIXIE
Oh, my God, Junie! Are you okay?!

JUNE
(deadpan)
Well, my rear end feels like someone's taken a blowtorch to
it, but I'll live.

TRIXIE
(visibly upset)
Oh, Junie!! I'm so sorry!! Why did you have to confess?!?!

JUNE
(angry and ashamed)
Because... paddlin' your sacrilegious rear end turns me on,
that's why!

TRIXIE
(emotions running the gamut)
What?!?!

JUNE
(in tears)
At first, I honestly believed that I was doin' it for your own
good, but then, after the first few times, I started soakin'
through my panties. That's when I knew I had to confess. I'm
so sorry, Trixie!! You must think I'm some kinda
d...degenerate!!

TRIXIE
(after a long pause)
Well..you already know what spankin' does to me, right?

JUNE
Yeah... so what?

TRIXIE
So, do you think I'm a degenerate?

JUNE
Of course not, Trixie. I may not understand why you enjoy
gettin' spanked so much, but that doesn't mean I think you're
a degenerate.

TRIXIE
(another long pause)
But, you know what I do out in the woods.

JUNE
Yeah.

TRIXIE
(just as she reaches JUNE'S front walkway)
So, maybe I oughta confess to bein' a pagan.

JUNE
Don't you even think about it! If those priests ever find out
what you've been doin' in the woods, they'll excommunicate
you!

TRIXIE
But, if I had confessed to bein' a pagan, instead of comin' to
you, then you wouldn't have felt the need to spank me, and if
you hadn't felt the need to spank me, then you wouldn't have
confessed to Father Allen.

                    JUNE
          (opening the front door)
    Come inside, Trixie. I have somethin' I wanna show you.

TRIXIE follows JUNE into the house, and closes the door behind
them. Once inside, both women shed their heels, and leave them
by the door. While passing through the foyer, JUNE stops and
turns her back to TRIXIE. Without another word, she proceeds
to reach beneath her skirts.

                    TRIXIE
          What are you doin', Junie?!

                    JUNE
          You'll see.

JUNE unfastens the garters from her stockings and rolls them
down, mouthing a silent prayer prior to peeling off her girdle

                    JUNE
          Hey, Trixie.

                    TRIXIE
          Yeah.

                    JUNE
    (grimacing as she tugs her girdle down from underneath her
                         slip)
    Remind me..never..to wear..a panty girdle..to confession!

                    TRIXIE
          (brimming with empathy)
          Oh, Junie! You poor thing!

Having liberated herself from the bondage of her delicates, JUNE bends over to grab the hems of her skirt and slip.

                    JUNE
              Brace yourself, Trix.

JUNE grimly lifts her skirts to reveal the fifteen mortifying emblems of her deftly-inflicted penance.

                    TRIXIE
              (gasping in horror)
    Oh, my God!! Junie!! Ohhhhhhhh!! You should see what that
              wicked priest did to you!!

                    JUNE
            (from beneath her skirts)
      I'm gonna have to take your word for it, hon.

                    TRIXIE
             (bursting into tears)
    Oh, my God, Junie! It's awful! I can't even imagine how much
                    it hurts!

                    JUNE
    You think my rear end looks bad, Trixie? Try to imagine what
      yours will look like once *you* confess to Father Allen!

                    TRIXIE
      I would do anything to keep him from hurtin' you, Junie!

JUNE
*(standing upright so that her dress falls down while turning
to face TRIXIE)*
I know you would, Trix, just promise me you won't go gettin'
any crazy ideas.

TRIXIE
(crossing her fingers)
I promise.

JUNE
What they don't know can't hurt us.

TRIXIE
Ayuh... Did Father Allen absolve you?

JUNE
Ayuh, right before he put the rod to my rear end for the
fifteenth goddamn time, he asked me whether or not I repented
for havin' spanked you.

TRIXIE
Oh, my God, really? What did you tell him?

JUNE
I told him I did.

TRIXIE
(trying not to sound too concerned)
...you're not gonna spank me anymore?

JUNE
What? Are you kiddin' me?! You're lucky I'm not spankin' you
now!

TRIXIE
But... you repented.

JUNE
I know.

TRIXIE
So, every time you spank me, you gotta confess all over again, right?

JUNE
(conspiratorially)
Not if you don't.

TRIXIE
(delighted with her friend's rationale)
What they don't know, can't hurt us!

JUNE
(still grinning)
You got it. Hey, Trix. Why don't you stay over here tonight

TRIXIE
(tearing up for no particular reason)
Really? That would be great!

JUNE
Ayuh. We can drink some wine and watch TV. Lucy's on tonight.

TRIXIE
I love Lucy!

JUNE
Me, too. Tell you what. You go and grab every pillow you can
find, and I'll get the first aid kit.

TRIXIE
Ooohh, it'll be like a slumber party!

JUNE
(rolling her eyes as she heads out of the room)
Yes, Trixie. Just like a slumber party.

TRIXIE
(tongue-in-cheek)
Hey, Junie! Aren't you gonna put your girdle back on?

JUNE
(with a wry grin)
Why? We're not goin' anywhere.

TRIXIE
(encouraged by JUNE'S sudden disregard for propriety)
Um..would it be okay if I..um..

JUNE
Oh, for God's sake, Trixie. Go ahead.

TRIXIE
(gleefully reaching up her skirt to shed her panties and
pantyhose)
Thanks, Junie!

JUNE
Sure. That'll make it easier for me to paddle you, tonight.

> TRIXIE
> (feigning protest)
> Hey!!

Both friends burst out laughing.

ACT OF ATTRITION

A Poem by Means of an Intermission

TIME: Approximately 3:30 PM the following Saturday

SETTING: The undercroft of Saint Michelle's Church

Trixie confesses to a grievous transgression
as she bends with her back to the minister's eye,
beseeching to keep him from swiftly upending
her over the kneeler with her dress hoisted high,
peeling her pantyhose down to her knees,
letting her underwear fall in the aisle,
paying her penance in spite of her pleas,
counting the strokes as she stares at the tile.

ACT THREE

TIME: An evening in July 1964, approximately 6:30 PM

SETTING: JUNE'S kitchen

Nearly eight months had passed since the Marine Corps had notified JUNE that her husband, Roy, had gone missing. While struggling to consider her husband's peril, JUNE begins to question many of the values that she has held throughout her life. During this time, she becomes even closer to TRIXIE, in spite of, or perhaps, because of, her friend's resolve to suffer corporal punishment in lieu of renouncing her pagan beliefs. Loath as she is to admit it, JUNE becomes increasingly curious about the ways in which TRIXIE and her "heathen friends" practice their devotion to the Lady of the Forest. After months of self-deliberation, JUNE finally agrees to attend a gathering of the Sacred Sisterhood of Flidais.

TRIXIE
(on the phone with JUNE)
I'm so excited that you're comin' tonight, Junie!

JUNE
Well, I gotta know what sort of mischief my best friend's been
gettin' herself into.

                    TRIXIE
                  (bemused)
Junie..Tonight's gatherin' is gonna be very special.

                    JUNE
              Really? Why's that?

                    TRIXIE
          We're initiatin' a new sister.

                    JUNE
                  (wryly)
              Ooh, lucky her.

                    TRIXIE
                 (reverent)
         It's a very sacred ceremony.

                    JUNE
    Oh, yeah? Is she gettin' her very own broom?

                    TRIXIE
               (exasperated)
                  Junie..

                    JUNE
I'm just teasin'..So, what should I wear to this *ceremony?*

                    TRIXIE
Oh, nothin' fancy. Just a nice, comfortable dress, but don't
bother wearin' nylons, we'll be goin' down to the beach.

                              JUNE
      Oh, yeah? Well, in that case, I'd better shave my legs. I
              don't wanna look like Magilla Gorilla.

                             TRIXIE
      Don't worry about that, Junie. These girls aren't gonna care.

                              JUNE
      What kind of girls go to a beach party without shavin' their
                              legs?

                             TRIXIE
                           You'll see.

About two hours later, TRIXIE arrives at JUNE'S house to find her friend ready and waiting. The air feels warm and humid as the two of them set off towards Casavant Beach. Within half an hour, they reach a clapboard walkway that winds through a dry salt marsh overgrown with tall grasses and low-lying shrubs. As they walk along, JUNE recalls tromping through the overgrowth with her sisters and playing hide-and-go-seek. The walkway eventually leads to the top of a gentle slope formed by cascading dunes of coarse, beige sand. JUNE follows TRIXIE for a long while, up and down the dunes, towards a secluded area of the beach, which lies beyond the summer cottages and house boats, well past the invasive glow of porch lights and street lamps, to a sunken cove that JUNE hasn't visited since she was a child. The absence of artificial lighting enables the two women to better appreciate the exceptionally large moon that shines overhead, amid a myriad of glimmering stars. Upon approaching their destination, JUNE notices a bonfire blazing in the distance, despite the fact that there is no one there to tend it.

JUNE
Hey, where is everybody?

TRIXIE
Oh, they'll be here, soon enough. It's still early.

JUNE
Well, I hope so. The tide's comin' in.

TRIXIE
(sighing)
Will you look at that moon.

JUNE
Ayuh, it almost seems blue.

TRIXIE
It sure does.

JUNE
Hey, Trix. My feet are killin' me. Do you think anyone would
mind if I took my shoes off?

TRIXIE
Of course not.

**JUNE slips off her shoes and wanders closer to the fire. The
intense heat soon compels her to stop about fifteen feet short
of the flames. While reveling in the warm glow, her eyes are
drawn to what appears to be a long, wooden plank, laying upon
the ground.**

JUNE
Hey, Trixie. Come take a look at this!

TRIXIE
(hurries over to JUNE)
I'm comin'!

JUNE
(handing the plank to TRIXIE)
I found it on the ground near the fire. It reminds me of the
paddle that Principal Lenehan used to keep in her desk.

TRIXIE
(with pride)
You mean, the board of correction?! No girl at Saint
Michelle's went before the board as often as I did!

JUNE
You mispronounced *bent,* Trixie.

TRIXIE
(with an impish grin)
Oh, did I?

JUNE
(laughing)
So, what's this thing for?

TRIXIE
Oh, that's for the initiation.

JUNE
Wait a minute. You mean, some girl's gonna get paddled,
tonight?

TRIXIE
Ayuh, that's how we initiate 'em.

JUNE
So, when you first joined this band of heathens, you had to
let them *spank* you?

TRIXIE
Ayuh.

JUNE
For Christ's sake, Trixie. Did it hurt?

TRIXIE
Oh God, yeah, but I got through it. Some girls can't even take
three strokes.

JUNE
Three strokes? Well, they wouldn't have lasted long in your
house.

TRIXIE
(giggling)
Nope.

JUNE
I mean, how bad can it be?

TRIXIE
Trust me, sis. It's like sittin' on a hornet's nest with your
panties down.

JUNE
Really?

                         TRIXIE
                        (solemnly)
                          Ayuh.

                          JUNE
            Well, if you can bear it, then, so can I.

                         TRIXIE
                        (giggling)
        I don't know, Junie. You're a lot more accustomed to givin'
                       than receivin'.

                          JUNE
        Yeah, maybe so, but my rear end can still take a beatin'. Tell
             you what. I'll let you try this thing out on me.

                         TRIXIE
        Oh, no, I couldn't do that. It's only meant to be used for the
                        initiation.

                          JUNE
             Oh, come on, Trix. I'm not gonna break it.

                         TRIXIE
                   I really shouldn't..

                          JUNE
        Please, Trixie! Just give me three good swats. Quick, before
                     your friends get here.

                         TRIXIE
                  (feigning apprehension)
           Oh, alright, but don't say I didn't warn you.

                    JUNE
                  I won't.

                   TRIXIE
  Okay. So, when a girl gets initiated, she has to kneel in the
        sand, with her back turned to the shore.

**Eager to show her friend that she's resilient enough to
withstand the paddle's sting, JUNE hurries to find a spot on
the beach that's relatively devoid of rocks, shells, and other
debris. About a minute later, she stops approximately fifty
feet from the approaching ocean's edge and kneels upon the
sand.**

                    JUNE
               (from a distance)
                  How's this?!

                   TRIXIE
       (walks over to JUNE and stops a few feet behind her)
                 That's fine, June!

                    JUNE
                Okay, what next?

                   TRIXIE
  Now, go ahead and lift your dress up above your waist.

                    JUNE
    (lifts her dress to reveal pale lavender panties underneath)
                    Okay.

                              TRIXIE
                 (reveling in her friend's submission)
               That's it. Now, pull down your panties.

                              JUNE
     For God's sake, Trixie! I'm not takin' down my underwear! What
                       if your friends show up?!

                              TRIXIE
          That's alright, Junie. A lot of girls can't complete the
     initiation because they're too scared to show their rear ends.

                              JUNE
                     (rubbing her bruised ego)
                    Hey, who said I was scared?!

                              TRIXIE
                         Well, you said..

                              JUNE
                          (indignant)
                    Fine. I'll take 'em down.

**Not to be outdone, JUNE slips her fingers inside the waistband
of her panties and tugs them down to her knees.**

                              JUNE
             There! Are you satisfied? Now, paddle me, already!

                              TRIXIE
             I will, as soon as you assume the position.

                              JUNE
                    Position? What position?!

                              TRIXIE
              You have to present yourself for the paddle.

                               JUNE
                           (exasperated)
              Oh, for the love of God, how do I do that?

                              TRIXIE
        Lift your dress up over your head and fall forward until your
                       hands touch the ground.

                               JUNE
                    You've got to be kiddin' me!

                              TRIXIE
                   Do you wanna do this, or not?

                               JUNE
                               Yes!

                              TRIXIE
          Then, hurry up! The other girls will be here any minute!

                               JUNE
                        Alright, alright!

JUNE turns the skirt of her dress inside out while bending at the waist so that it hangs down over her head. The sharp downward slope of the shoreline props JUNE'S bottom to such an extent that Mother Nature appears to be conspiring against her.

                         JUNE
       Trixie, this is ridiculous. I can't see a damn thing.

                        TRIXIE
       That's okay, hon. It won't hurt as much if you can't see
                     what's comin'.

                         JUNE
                    (mildly alarmed)
                   Well, that's a relief.

                        TRIXIE
       You know, Junie. I really don't feel right about this.

                         JUNE
       Oh, come on, Trixie. I didn't get half undressed for nothin'!
       Besides, you know I wouldn't think twice about paddlin' your
                     sorry behind.

                        TRIXIE
         (feigning apprehension in order to stall for time)
                      I know, but..

Just then, TRIXIE turns around and waves to a point near the summit of the windswept sands. That same moment, nearly two dozen barefoot women wearing loose-fitting, paisley print dresses rise up from the dunes. Swiftly and silently, they descend upon TRIXIE and JUNE. The group is led by EILEEN LENEHAN, the former principal of Saint Michelle's Catholic Girls School. EILEEN is a woman of nondescript appearance and average build, with piercing hazel eyes and fine gray hair that hangs halfway down her back. As her entourage approaches,

EILEEN seems delighted to find JUNE in such a fittingly compromised position.

JUNE
(well within earshot of EILEEN and the other women)
Go ahead, Trixie! What are you waitin' for? Just pretend you're Principal Lenehan, and I'm some shameless hussy who's been called down to your office.

TRIXIE
Alright, if you say so, Junie.

EILEEN
(clearing her throat for dramatic effect)
June Marie Jenkins! What did I say would happen if I ever caught you with your skirts up at recess again?!

JUNE
(startled by TRIXIE'S ability to mimic Principal Lenehan but all too happy to play along)
Oh, I'm sorry, Ma'am. It's just... well, Brendan DuPont said that he'd give me somethin' sweet if I showed him my bottom, and so, I did.

EILEEN
(barely able to stifle her laughter)
Miss Jenkins, I am shocked and appalled! Is that how young ladies ought to behave?

JUNE
(trying to sound remorseful)
No, Ma'am.

TRIXIE
Well, by the time I'm through with you, you'll be too
embarrassed to show your bottom to anybody!

JUNE
(trying to sound fretful)
Are you gonna punish me, Ma'am?

TRIXIE and EILEEN exchange conspiratorial grins.

TRIXIE
Young lady, I'm going to paddle your rear end until you can't
sit for a week!

JUNE
(trying not to laugh)
Oh, no! Please, Principal Lenehan! Not the paddle!

EILEEN
(barely able to contain herself)
Hush, now, or you'll get it twice as long!

JUNE
(melodramatic)
Oh, no! Pleeeeease, Principal Lenehan!

EILEEN
(with real authority)
I said **hush**!

JUNE
(startled by the conviction with which TRIXIE plays her role)
...Wow, Trixie! You sound *just* like that **old witch**!

                              TRIXIE
                  (preying upon her friend's gullibility)
                         Gee, thanks, Junie.

                               JUNE
            Now, let's see if you can swing a paddle like her!

                              TRIXIE
                         Okay, I'll try..

With a wink and nod, TRIXIE hands the paddle to EILEEN. Much to the amusement of all those in attendance, the former principal takes several exaggerated practice swings before striking the heart of JUNE'S bottom.

                               JUNE
          (instantly reacquainted with the paddle's wicked sting)
                Owwwwwww!! Holy Mother of God! That hurts!!

EILEEN rolls her eyes at JUNE'S blasphemous protest and proceeds to administer another firm stroke.

                               JUNE
                     Owwwwwww!! Jesus Christ!!

TRIXIE can barely keep herself from laughing as EILEEN rears back to paddle JUNE for a third time.

                               JUNE
         Aaaaaaagggghhh!! Okay, Trixie! That's enough! I surrender!

TRIXIE rushes over to face JUNE as EILEEN prepares to strike her friend's already reddened bottom, yet again.

                    TRIXIE
        (standing directly in front of JUNE)
              You okay, Junie?

                    JUNE
   *(pulling the dress back over her head so she can look at
                    TRIXIE)*
   Yeah, I'm alright, but you weren't kiddin' about that thing!

                    TRIXIE
        Stings somethin' awful, doesn't it?

                    JUNE
   (an instant before and after the paddle finds its mark)
              It sure does..
   Owwwwwwwwww!! Damn it, Trixie! I said, that's enough!

                    TRIXIE
              (playing innocent)
            I didn't do anything.

                    JUNE
   Well, if you didn't paddle me just now, then who the hell
                    did?!

                    EILEEN
              (heartily)
         Blessed be, June Marie!

**JUNE immediately recognizes the older woman's voice to be that
of EILEEN LENEHAN. She can't believe that straight-laced,
church-going EILEEN could be involved with a pagan cult.**

                    JUNE
                 (mortified)
         Oh, my God.. Principal Lenehan??

                   EILEEN
                 (cheerful)
        June Marie Jenkins! Well, how are you?

                    JUNE
          (desperately trying to save face)
     More than a bit embarrassed, Ma'am, and very sore at the
     moment. If you don't mind my askin', how long have you been
                     paddlin' me?

                   EILEEN
     Oh, from the time you were in kindergarten, I imagine.

THE SISTERHOOD bursts into laughter.

                    JUNE
                 (chagrined)
     You got me there, Ma'am. I'm sorry you and these other ladies
     have to see me like this. Trixie and I were just playin'.

                   EILEEN
     Oh, no need to apologize, sweetie. It's certainly not the
                 first time, now is it?

                    JUNE
           (blushing at both ends)
                 No, Ma'am.

EILEEN
I'm actually quite pleased to find you in this position.

JUNE
Um... you are?

EILEEN
Why yes, June. I had Trixie bring you here tonight, because we
have some very important matters to discuss.

JUNE
Oh.. well, it doesn't seem polite for me to have my back
turned when we're havin' a discussion.

EILEEN
Oh, no, Junie. Stay right where you are. You and I are just
gettin' started.

JUNE
(nervously)
We are?

EILEEN
(assuming a more serious tone)
Why, yes. I hear you acquired my mother's antique hairbrush a
while back.

JUNE
(giggling nervously)
Oh, yes. I bought it at her estate sale.

EILEEN
Ah, my dear old Mum. Tough as nails, she was.

JUNE
God rest her soul.

EILEEN
How's that brush workin' for you, June Marie?

JUNE
(unnerved by the question)
Oh, um..it works just fine. Keeps my
hair from goin' astray.

EILEEN
That's good to hear. Does it do the same for Trixie Ann?

JUNE
I don't know what you mean, Ma'am.

EILEEN
Do you think Trixie has gone astray?

JUNE
(responding in spite of herself)
Y-yes.

EILEEN
Why is that?

JUNE
Because she's broken the First Commandment. And I'm afraid
that if the priests find out that she worships false gods,
they'll excommunicate her. Trixie has always been a good
Catholic.

97

EILEEN

(subdued at the outset, growing more impassioned towards the end)

Yes, she most certainly has, June. Tell me, what does it mean to be a good Catholic? Does it mean persecuting your lifelong friend for believing in a healthy, humane way of living; one that existed thousands of years before the advent of Christianity?! Does it mean letting a sadistic priest beat our mothers, our sisters, and us, for decades, under the false pretense of absolving your sins?! You know, June, my mother raised me to believe that I'd lose my soul if she wasn't beatin' my rear end all the time, and so, I learned to ask for the hairbrush, and I learned to take pleasure in my punishments. I learned to hate myself for loving my body and for loving other women's bodies. I learned to crave the rod of correction in order to relieve my guilt, but when I confessed to enjoying it, the priests condemned me for being a degenerate, and so, I was damned if I did, and I was damned if I didn't. That's why I resigned from Saint Michelle's, and renounced the Church. I simply couldn't be an accomplice to the traumatization of young women and girls any longer. I, like most of these women here, chose to serve the Lady of the Forest so that we could experience pleasure and pain on our terms, without fearing for our safety or our salvation.

Nearly a minute passes before JUNE speaks again.

JUNE

(respectfully)

Ms. Lenehan, why did you have Trixie bring me here, tonight?

EILEEN

You know, June. Your mother and I have been friends for a long time.

                         JUNE
          Yes, Ms. Lenehan. She's said as much.

                        EILEEN
Whenever I would come over for a visit, she and I would spend
           hours talking about you and your sisters.

                         JUNE
Yes, Ma'am. My sisters and I often had trouble sittin' shortly
                    after those visits.

                        EILEEN
                      (chuckling)
Oh, dear. Well, I'm sorry for any discomfort I might have
caused, but there isn't much your mother hasn't told me about
    you girls, and there isn't much I wouldn't tell her.

                         JUNE
                   (growing nervous)
            No, Ma'am. I don't imagine there is.

                        EILEEN
Tell me, Trixie Ann. What do you suppose June's parents would
  do if they found out that she had been spanking you with a
    hairbrush, each and every week, for well over a year?

                        TRIXIE
                   (with enthusiasm)
Oh, they'd have a fit! Why, I bet they'd put Junie over the
front fence, and take turns strappin' her bare bottom, every
                    day, for a month!
         Ayuh, I bet that's just what they'd do!

                              EILEEN
Oh, my word, Trixie. Surely, you can't be serious. June is a
grown woman, after all. June, please tell me your friend is
                          exaggerating.

                               JUNE
                            (ruefully)
                    I'm afraid not, Ms. Lenehan.

                              EILEEN
Well, then, young lady. Can you give me one good reason why I
shouldn't tell your parents about what you've been doing to
                          poor Trixie?

                               JUNE
    (pleading ignorance in a vain attempt to avoid disgrace)
                 What I've been doin' to her, Ma'am?

                              EILEEN
                            (sternly)
Do you or do you not derive carnal pleasure from spanking your
                    friend with a hairbrush?!

                               JUNE
                      (in a trembling voice)
                          Um, well, I..

                              EILEEN
                         (with authority)
                    Answer me, June Marie!

                           JUNE
                  (overcome with shame)
     Yes! Yes! Oh, God, Trixie! I'm so sorry! I'm so, so sorry!!
                  (breaks down sobbing)

                          TRIXIE
             (rushing over to comfort her friend)
     Shhhhh..It's alright, Junie! I forgive you. Everything's gonna
                        be alright.

                           JUNE
                    (still sobbing)
                   I'm sorry, Trixie!

**TRIXIE stays by JUNE and continues to comfort her. EILEEN
remains silent for a long while before addressing TRIXIE.**

                          EILEEN
     Trixie, I'm going to let you decide whether or not I ought to
        speak with June's parents about the trespasses she has
                     committed against you.

                          TRIXIE
     Oh, please don't, Ma'am. June isn't the only one who's guilty
                of indulging in my punishments.

                          EILEEN
      I see. Very well, then. I shall not speak to her parents
     regarding this matter, provided that she agrees to take two
                           vows.

                         JUNE
                      (sniffling)
I-I'll do anythin' to keep you from notifyin' my parents, Ms.
                      Lenehan.

                        EILEEN
First, promise me that you will never again subject Trixie to
          corporal punishment against her will.

                         JUNE
                     I promise.

                        EILEEN
Second, promise me that you will never betray her affiliation
      with this secret society to another living soul.

                         JUNE
               I promise, Ms. Lenehan.

                        EILEEN
Understand that if you break either of these vows, I will tell
your parents that you have taken carnal pleasure in spanking
  your dearest friend, and I will tell Father Allen that you
             have been cavorting with pagans.

                         JUNE
                     (shuddering)
               I understand, Ma'am.

                        EILEEN
Now, to ensure that you keep your vows, each of the sisters
  gathered here tonight will give you a reminder with the
                        paddle.

                    JUNE
                 (panicking)
       How many sisters are there, Ms. Lenehan?

                   EILEEN
                (cheerfully)
         Not including myself, twenty-two.

                    JUNE
*(shuddering at the thought of what lay in store for her rear
                     end)*
                 Oh, my God!

                   EILEEN
           Trixie Ann, you may begin.

                   TRIXIE
                 Yes, Ma'am.

                    JUNE
           No, wait! You can't do this!

                   EILEEN
       Would you prefer that I tell your parents?

                    JUNE
              No! Please, don't!

                   EILEEN
   Then, you must agree to accept this punishment in full, as
   retribution for the physical and emotional anguish that you
                 have caused Trixie.

                    JUNE
          (tearfully resigned to her fate)
                   Y-yes.

*Seconds later, the paddle slices through the air with an
audible whoosh, as TRIXIE administers a searing stroke to
JUNE'S bare backside. TRIXIE then passes the paddle to the
woman who is next in line, and so it continues, for well over
fifteen minutes. JUNE'S subsequent cries of distress are
mercifully baffled by the roar of the rising tide. In between
shrieks and wails, she is struck by the kind and caring way in
which each of the women address her. "We're all so proud
of you, June." "You're being very brave." "I know it hurts,
but it'll be over, soon." Many of the voices sound disarmingly
familiar. The tide is very high by the time the last woman in
line administers the final stroke. JUNE remains in position
for a long time following her punishment, until all of her
shame and guilt have been wept away. EILEEN waits several more
minutes before speaking to her again.*

                   EILEEN
June Marie Jenkins. You are hereby initiated into the Sacred
            Sisterhood of Flidais.

                    JUNE
        W...what? I don't understand.

                   EILEEN
We welcome you to join us. You, of course, are free to decline
our invitation, but I do hope that you'll consider it, as I
       have a special duty in mind for you.

                    JUNE
        (gradually regaining her composure)
                 A..a duty?

                   EILEEN
I need someone who is willing and able to administer corporal
punishment to any member of The Sisterhood who feels that she
              has fallen short of our standards.

                    JUNE
   So, some of these girls have been *askin'* for it, huh?

                   EILEEN
Not some of them, June. *All* of them, and if you agree to join
              us, they'll all be asking you.

                    JUNE
                 (swooning)
                   Me?

                   EILEEN
              Yes, June Marie.

**EILEEN gently helps JUNE to her feet. JUNE reaches down to
discover that her underwear is missing.**

                   TRIXIE
                 (grinning)
   I got your panties, June. Trust me, you'll be better off
               without 'em, tonight.

                    JUNE
                 (mortified)
             Oh, my God, Trixie.

                              EILEEN
Don't fret, sweetie. We're all girls, here. Now, come and meet
                        your new sisters.

JUNE lets her dress fall so that it covers her thoroughly paddled bottom, and slowly turns around to face the gathering, at which point, she is astounded to discover nearly two dozen women of every age, shape, and size standing by the bonfire. As the flames illuminate their gentle faces, JUNE marvels at how many of them she recognizes. Among those in attendance are housewives, waitresses, nurses, and nuns. JUNE looks at all of these women, several of whom are old enough to be her mother, and swoons at the thought of tending to their upturned bottoms.

                               JUNE
                    (trying to sound dignified)
      Ms. Lenehan, I humbly accept your invitation to join The
                           Sisterhood.

                              EILEEN
     Blessed be, June Marie Jenkins. The Sisterhood welcomes you.
      May I presume that you also accept the duty with which I have
                           assigned you?

                               JUNE
               (barely able to contain her enthusiasm)
                         Yes, Ma'am. I do.

                              TRIXIE
    Excellent. Just remember, June. You can only provide incentive
      to those who specifically request it. In addition, you must
     exercise restraint when determining the severity of any given
                      punishment. Is that understood?

                              JUNE
                          Yes, Ma'am.

                             EILEEN
                  (addressing THE SISTERHOOD)
        Sisters, let it be known that if you decide to consult with
        June, you agree to accept whatever incentive she prescribes,
                    in full. Is that understood?

                          THE SISTERHOOD
                          Yes, Ma'am.

                             EILEEN
        So be it. Trixie Ann LaFleur, in order to ensure that June is
        available to perform her duties, I must prohibit you from
                seeking her incentive more than once per week.

                             TRIXIE
                          Yes, Ma'am.

                              JUNE
        Better make that twice a week, Ms. Lenehan. Trixie tends to
                      need a lot of... *incentive.*

THE SISTERHOOD bursts into laughter.

                             EILEEN
        Well, if you're certain that you'll be able to fulfill your
            obligations to the other members of The Sisterhood.

                              JUNE
                    Yes, Ma'am. Quite certain.

EILEEN
Very well, then. I'll allow it.

TRIXIE turns to see JUNE grinning from ear to ear.

EILEEN
Let us adjourn for tonight. Blessed be, sisters.

THE SISTERHOOD
Blessed be.

END

ABOUT THE AUTHOR

Lee Todd Lacks seeks to blur the distinctions between rants, chants, anecdotes, and anthems. His experience of living with significant vision and hearing deficits often informs his writing and artwork, which have appeared in *The Monarch Review, The Quarterday Review, Crack The Spine Anthology, Vine Leaves Literary Journal, Bop Dead City, Liquid Imagination,* and elsewhere. In December of 2016, Fermata Publishing released his first chapbook of poetry and short fiction, entitled *Underneath.* In May of 2017, Lee Todd presented selections of his poetry at Stanford University's Center for Computer Research in Music and Acoustics (CCRMA) in collaboration with a group of multimedia artists from the United States and Romania.

Other HellBound Books Titles

Available at: www.hellboundbookspublishing.com

Depraved Desires: Volume 1

Desires.
We all have them, even if we won't admit it. Some are considered normal, and probably healthy. But what about the others?

Those haunting stirrings within that rail against societal norms and the bounds of decency?

Depraved Desires delves into the writhing depths of carnal appetites and sin, peeling back the veneer to reveal tales of wanton lust and supernatural depravity... The terrifying prospect of knife play; a cosmic liaison; a classy party that turned out to be more than a hired call girl ever expected; or when a sinister fantasy becomes reality - all will shock you.

Whether your desires drive you mad or your madness drives your desires, delving within these pages will take you to places where those itches live, the ones that demand to be scratched.

Depraved Desires: Volume 2

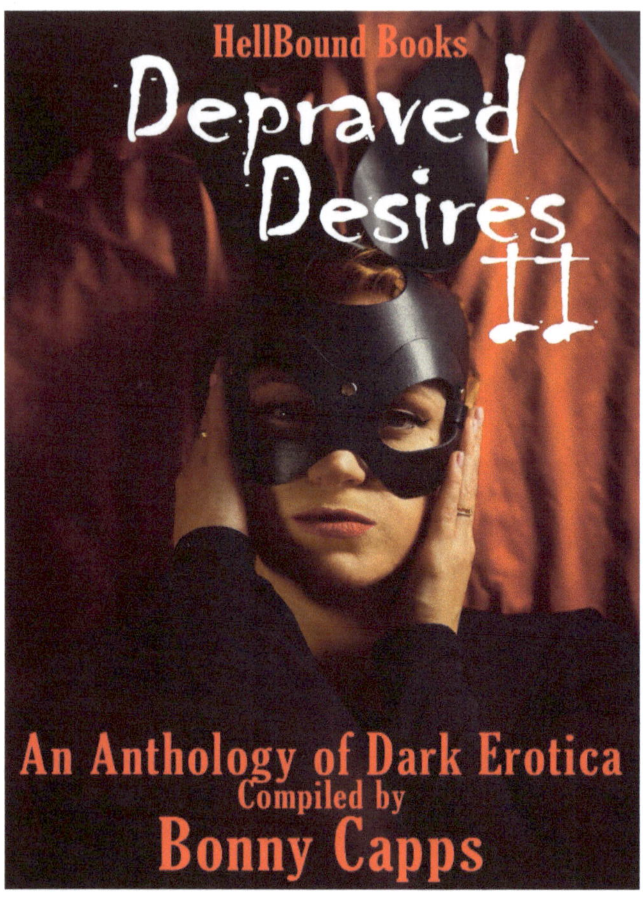

A dark and wonderfully stimulating collection of the disturbingly erotic from the very best authors in the business - all lovingly selected by the internationally renowned authoress Bonnie Capps.

Sixteen mouthwateringly delectable tales from: Duana Monroe, Jacob Mielke, Matt Payne, Ken Goldman, M.J. Sutton, D. Norfolk, Mawr Gorshin, J. Stanley, Tim J. Finn, Shane Porteous, J.L. Boekestein, Becky & Lee Narron, Marela Aryan Ballot, Becky Narron & J.L. Boekestein and Jennifer Lynne

The Pleasure Hunt

After meeting the mysterious *Dark Dance* on the casual encounters website, The Pleasure Hunters Club, *Sexy Cupid* finds himself enchanted by a enigmatic seductress – *Dark Dance*.

After experiencing bizarre, nightmarish visions during their first physical liaison, *Cupid* awakes on a bench somewhere in Louisville, unable to get the mystifying creature off his mind. As he begins to search both online and through the seedy streets of the city for her, he uncovers harrowing truths about the object of his obsession, truths which fill him with both indomitable dread and inexplicable love for her.

By the time *Cupid* begins to understand the terror he faces, the shackles on his soul are already too tight as the ancient monster has her talons dug well into his flesh.

Every time he is swept away to her world of Theia - the Moon Realm - she extracts and devours yet another piece of his very essence, and despite the merciless torment of his encounters with his obsession - and the warnings of, a menacing stranger - he presses on to find her, dragging himself deeper into her darkened realm.

Cupid soon finds that he may have but one opportunity to escape the demonic *Dark Dance*, but the bewitchment she has cast upon his heart may deter him from making a stand; with his soul about to slip down the gullet of the beast, *Cupid* has to make a decision before he is forever wrapped in the wicked thaumaturge's wings of eternal damnation.

The Waning

Beatrix woke up in a small metal cage, Lost in the darkness, a persistent dripping sound her only company.

She was celebrating a promotion that was the culmination of her entire ruthless, driven career; a promotion that would cement her status enough for her to take her relationship with her girlfriend out of the lesbian closet; Beatrix had finally made it.

And then she was here, disoriented and petrified in a blackness she could not define. Yet the reality of her Master may be even more terrifying than the crushing darkness and enveloping isolation. He appears as an ominous shadow in the doorway of her cell, never speaking. Instead, he teaches Beatrix the language of pain and torture, of submission and obedience, of domination and possession

With each passing day, the fight and hope in Beatrix begins to shrivel and wane. With each savage beating, her survivalist instincts rise up to overwhelm the person she was. With each dehumanizing condition, she begins to forget who she was and the life from which she was ripped.

Can Beatrix ward off the psychological breakdown of her Master? Can she resist the temptation to survive and thrive through submission? Either Beatrix will succeed at surviving and escaping the torments of her Master or her Master will succeed at breaking her completely and reforming her into his design for a human possession…

A HellBound Books LLC Publication

www.hellboundbookspublishing.com

Printed in the United States of America